Families

Jennifer Nowak

Rosen
REAL
READERS

Rosen Classroom Books & Materials
New York

Families can eat together.

Families can work together.

Families can read together.

Families can play together.

Families can go to the store together.

What do you like to do with your family?

Words to Know

play

read

store